BIG AND BAD

Walter Lorraine (wh) Books

www.houghtonmifflinbooks.com

Library of Congress Cataloging-in-Publication Data
Delessert, Etienne.
Big and Bad / Etienne Delessert.
p. cm.
"Walter Lorraine books."
Summary: In this variation on the classic tale of the three little pigs,
two clever cats decide to rid their locale of a vicious wolf whose
hunger threatens the entire planet, and enlist the help of assorted
animals to build houses for the bait—three exquisitely pink pigs.
ISBN-13: 978-0-618-88934-1
ISBN-10: 0-618-88934-5
[1. Wolves—Fiction. 2. Animals—Fiction. 3. Greed—Fiction.] I. Title.
PZ7.D3832Big 2008
[E]—dc22
                              2007019291

Printed in SINGAPORE
TWP 10 9 8 7 6 5 4 3 2 1

BIG AND BAD

ETIENNE DELESSERT

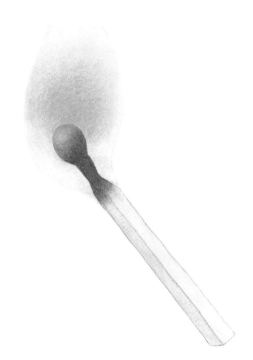

Houghton Mifflin Company Boston 2008

Walter Lorraine Books

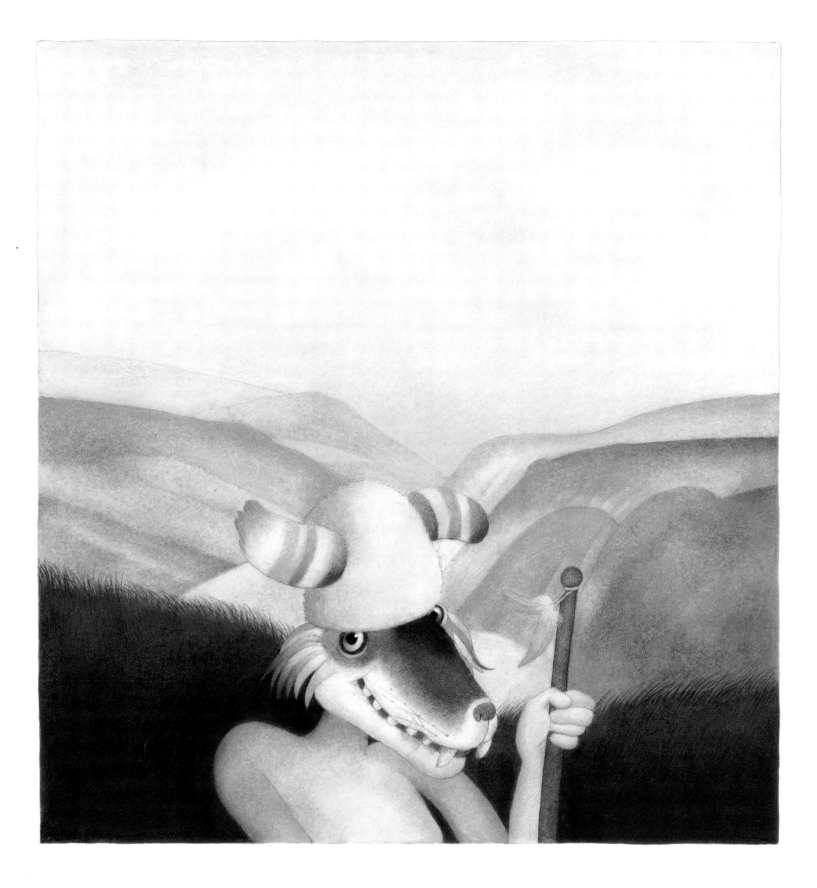

Wolf ran over the hills,

lean, mean, and

always hungry.

He came from far away,

so nobody understood a word

of what he said.

Soon he grew taller than the

midnight moon.

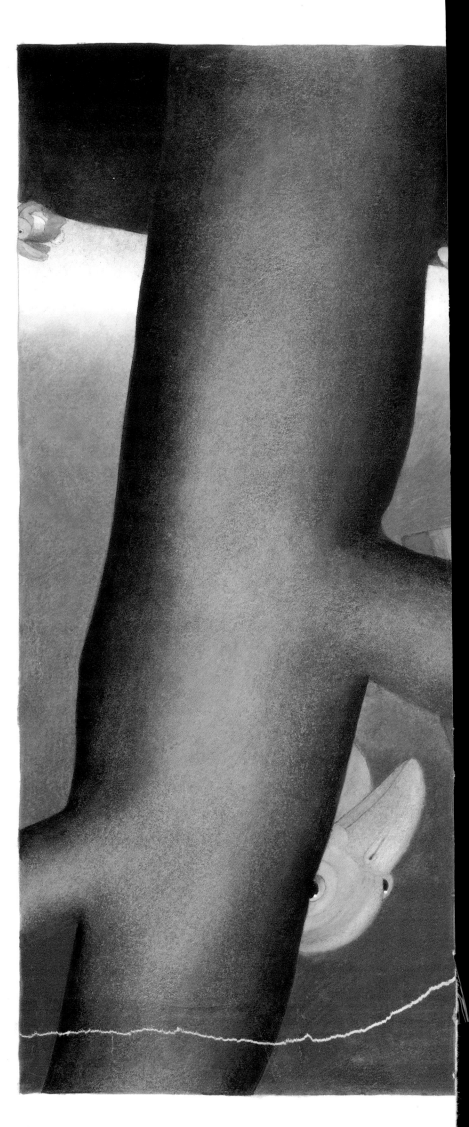

He slept late, sang so loud
that rabbits ran in circles,
mice and moles jumped into their holes,
birds tucked their heads under their wings,
and cows' milk turned sour.

When Wolf wasn't hunting
he was making splendid hats
with the fur of animals he
had gobbled down.
His head was so large that he needed
the skin of seven cats to cover it.

After every meal a flock of birds

fluttered into Big and Bad's open mouth

to clean his gruesomely shiny teeth.

Beavers tried to drown Wolf in their pond, crows pelted him with walnuts, thousands of moles dug a giant trap underground, but nothing could stop his feeding spree.

"Soon," snapped a fox, "the planet will be too small for his appetite."

Two cats, marauding in the valley,
decided to try to stop the predator.
Watching some pigs playing in
the tall grass, they devised a plan
to trap the Wolf.

"These plump little pigs are so cute,"
said one of the cats.
"Their soft skin, such an exquisite shade
of pink, will make Big and Bad shiver
with pleasure."

The cats summoned all the animals
of the hill:
"Our charming friends need help
building a house to protect them
from Wolf's sharp teeth."

The next morning, while Big and Bad slept, hundreds of birds began to build the house of straw and twigs.

The little pigs clapped as the birds and a badger carefully wove the walls and dug a hideout with a trapdoor. They all were happy to be part of the secret plan!

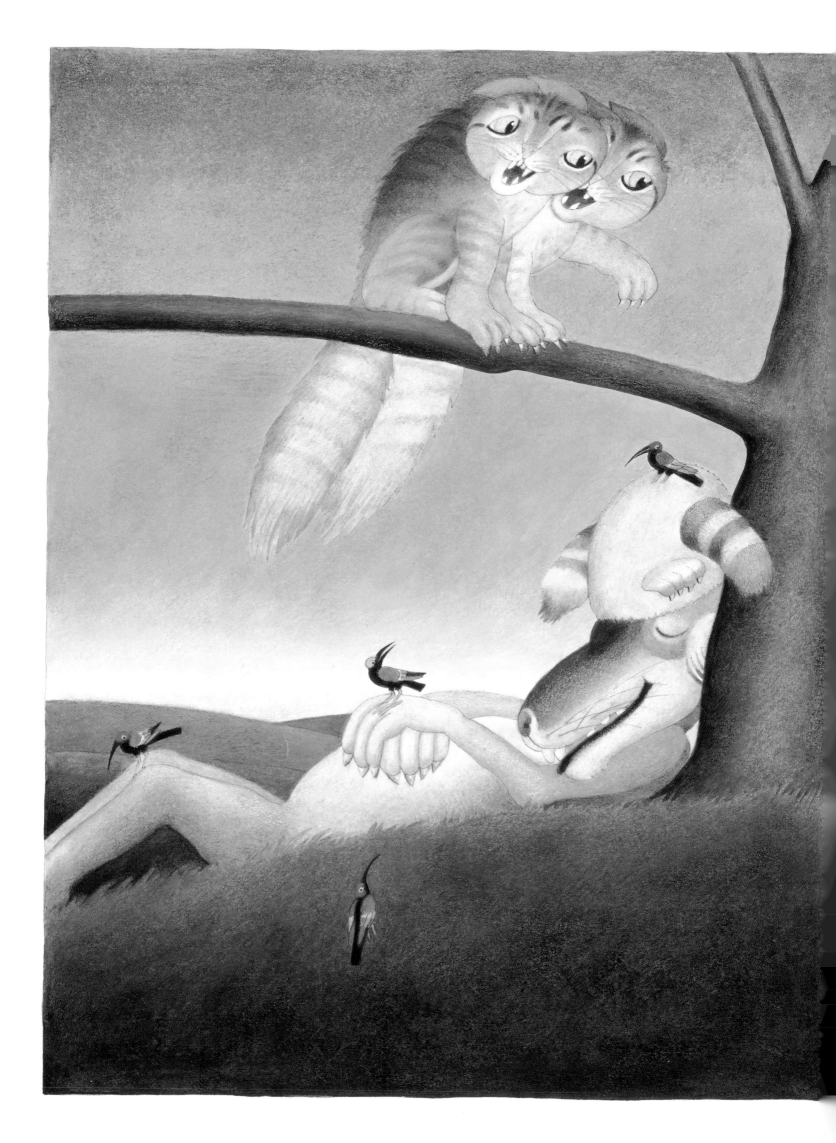

At midday the cats climbed a tree

near Wolf, woke him up with

a screeching song, and then darted

as fast as they could to the hut.

Wolf had just enough time

to see them disappear inside

with the three pigs.

Big and Bad put his fur hat on

and trotted down the hill.

"I am going to swallow these

sweet little pigs in one gulp

and skin those beautiful cats:

what a great hat they'll make."

Wolf stood in front of the house,

inhaled a huge amount of fresh air,

and—huff and puff!—he blew away

the twigs and straw. The hut

vanished in a dusty storm.

Surprise! There was no one home!

Wolf climbed a high rock and

screamed a terrible scream.

Then he rushed through the forest

to find someone to put into

his stomach.

The next day the cats invited a gang
of beavers to help the pigs build a
cabin of logs. Once the roof was
in place, the cats went to the sleeping
Wolf and sang their shrill song
once again.

Wolf galloped down the hill
just in time to see the cats and the
adorable little pigs close the door
of their new home on him.
Big and Bad circled the house
stealthily before smashing the
door with his shoulder.
No one home!

Wolf jumped onto the tall rock
and howled some very angry words
that no one understood.

The next afternoon the cats let
Wolf sleep late. Waking around
three, he could see the pigs
frolicking in the tall grass,
waving at him and blowing kisses,
before hiding under the hat he
had left behind. Wolf spit with rage,
and the little pigs vanished in the fields.

Once again the cats gathered all
the animals of the hill and built a
handsome brick house for the pigs.

Wolf slept under his tree,
dreaming of the tender little pigs,
their skin an exquisite shade of pink,
laughing at him as they danced
under the pale moon.

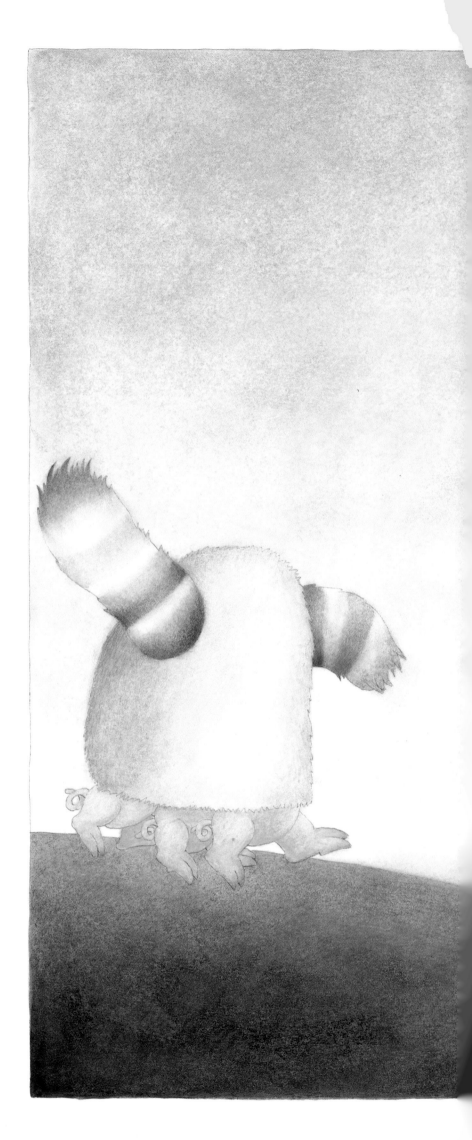

Down by the stream Wolf found
the brick house with a pig at each
window, two cats bowling with an
armadillo in the front yard, and
a beaver teasing him in the sun
of the late afternoon while cleaning
his teeth with a sharp twig.

With a formidable cry Wolf flew
down the hill just in time to see
the cats lock the heavy door.
Big and Bad circled the house,
sniffing and growling. He soon
realized that the walls were so
well built, he could not bring
them down.

He got a whiff of a sweet, spicy scent
rising from the chimney.

"Hey," thought Wolf, "I bet the cats
are cooking one of those little round
pigs just for me!"

So he climbed up on the roof,
took a deep breath, slipped down
the chimney, and fell into the middle
of a wild fire.

With a most horrible wail, the burning
Wolf shot out into the evening skies.

You can still see Wolf

circling around the earth

as bright as a shooting star.